It Looked
Like Spilt Milk

by Charles G. Shaw

SCHOLASTIC INC.

New York   Toronto   London   Auckland   Sydney

ISBN 0-590-42875-6

All rights reserved. Published by Scholastic Inc.,
730 Broadway, New York, NY 10003, by arrangement with
Harper & Row, Publishers, Inc.

12 11 10 9 8 7 6 5 4 3 2 1   9/8 0 1 2 3 4/9

Printed in the U.S.A.   23

First Scholastic printing, September 1989

Sometimes it looked
like Spilt Milk.
But it wasn't Spilt Milk.

Sometimes it looked
like a Rabbit.
But it wasn't a Rabbit.

Sometimes it looked
like a Bird.
But it wasn't a Bird.

Sometimes it looked

like a Tree.

But it wasn't a Tree.

Sometimes it looked
  like an Ice Cream Cone.
But it wasn't an Ice Cream Cone.

Sometimes it looked

like a Flower.

But it wasn't a Flower.

Sometimes it looked
like a Pig.
But it wasn't a Pig.

Sometimes it looked
   like a Birthday Cake.
But it wasn't a Birthday Cake.

Sometimes it looked
like a Sheep.
But it wasn't a Sheep.

Sometimes it looked
like a Great Horned Owl.
But it wasn't a Great Horned Owl.

Sometimes it looked

like a Mitten.

But it wasn't a Mitten.

Sometimes it looked
like a Squirrel.
But it wasn't a Squirrel.

Sometimes it looked
like an Angel.
But it wasn't an Angel.

Sometimes it looked
like Spilt Milk.
But it wasn't Spilt Milk.

It was just a Cloud in the Sky.